Dear Parent:
Your child's love of

Every child learns to read in a different way and at his or her own speed. Some go back and forth between reading levels and read favorite books again and again. Others read through each level in order. You can help your young reader improve and become more confident by encouraging his or her own interests and abilities. From books your child reads with you to the first books he or she reads alone, there are I Can Read Books for every stage of reading:

SHARED READING
Basic language, word repetition, and whimsical illustrations, ideal for sharing with your emergent reader

BEGINNING READING
Short sentences, familiar words, and simple concepts for children eager to read on their own

READING WITH HELP
Engaging stories, longer sentences, and language play for developing readers

READING ALONE
Complex plots, challenging vocabulary, and high-interest topics for the independent reader

ADVANCED READING
Short paragraphs, chapters, and exciting themes for the perfect bridge to chapter books

I Can Read Books have introduced children to the joy of reading since 1957. Featuring award-winning authors and illustrators and a fabulous cast of beloved characters, I Can Read Books set the standard for beginning readers.

A lifetime of discovery begins with the magical words **"I Can Read!"**

Visit www.icanread.com for information
on enriching your child's reading experience.

I Can Read Book® is a trademark of HarperCollins Publishers.

Batman: I Am Batman
Copyright © 2016 DC Comics.
BATMAN and all related characters and elements are trademarks of and © DC Comics.
(s16)

HARP35807
Library of Congress Control Number: 2015961041
ISBN 978-0-06-236087-8

Book design by Victor Joseph Ochoa
16 17 18 19 20 LSCC 10 9 8 7 6 5 4 3 ❖ First Edition

I Can Read! READING 2 WITH HELP

by Delphine Finnegan
pictures by Andie Tong

Batman created by Bob Kane with Bill Finger

HARPER
An Imprint of HarperCollinsPublishers

My name is Bruce Wayne.

I live in Gotham City.

I own Wayne Enterprises.

We build the best high-tech gadgets.

We make everything from huge planes
to the smallest computers.

This work is important to me.

I drive the best cars.

I use the newest gadgets.

I need these tools

day *and* night.

When I get home,

I head to a secret cave.

It is deep underground.

I keep watch over Gotham City.
My butler, Alfred, helps
keep my identity secret.

"Sir, you'll want to see this,"

says Alfred.

It is the Bat-Signal!

The Gotham City police send

this signal when they need my help.

My Batsuit and cape protect me.

My Utility Belt holds lots of gadgets.

I wear a mask

so no one knows who I am.

I jump into the Batmobile
and race into the night.

I contact Commissioner Gordon.
He is in charge
of Gotham City's police force.
"Something funny is happening
at the museum," he says.

When I arrive,

I see a poster about a new exhibit.

The rarest jewels

will be on display.

The show opens tomorrow.

I also see something strange.

The museum doors are wide open.

The alarm is broken.

All of the guards are gone.

I head to the main hall

and find the guards.

"This should do the trick," I say.

Suddenly, a net falls down.

"Trick's on you, Batman!"

It's the Riddler!

He's not alone.

Catwoman and the Joker

make it a trio of trouble.

I twist and turn.
I try to get unstuck
from the net
while the three thieves
pack their bags.

I get free and grab my Batarangs.

Zip!

One slices the rope.

Zap!

I throw the other at the Riddler.

It stops him in his tracks.

But the Joker and Catwoman

get away.

"Call Commissioner Gordon.

Tell him I'll get this duo soon,"

I shout to the guards.

Then I follow the two fiends.

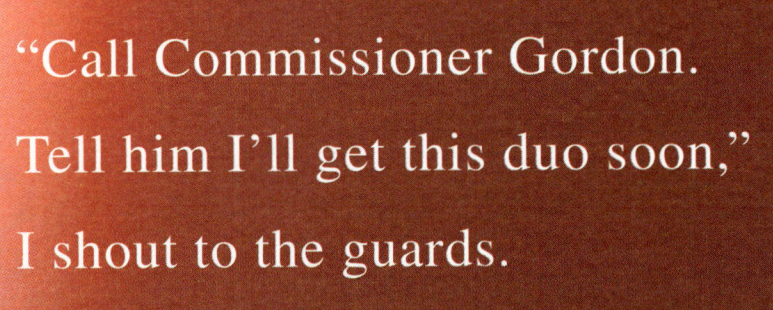

The Joker hitches a ride

from his crew.

Catwoman runs the other way.

"You have to pick a path,"

calls Catwoman.

I toss a tracer

at the Joker's helicopter.

It's a direct hit.

Then I follow Catwoman.

I chase her until

there is nowhere left to go.

Cats don't like water.

"You're cornered, Catwoman!"

I say.

Two down, one to go.

It is time to deal with the Joker.

I get into the Batmobile

and take off.

I check the tracer.

It locates the Joker.

He is hiding in the hills.

The Joker throws a party

at his hilltop hideaway.

He shows his loot to his crew.

He tells joke after joke.

I wait for the right time to strike.

"Who invited this party crasher?" shouts the Joker.

"Time to tie up some loose ends," I reply.

The Gotham City police arrive.

The trio of trouble

will be safely behind bars

and the jewels will return

to the museum.

I head out into the night.

Gotham City needs my help.

I will *always* answer the call.

I am Batman!

Dear Parent:
Your child's love of reading starts here!

Every child learns to read in a different way and at his or her own speed. Some go back and forth between reading levels and read favorite books again and again. Others read through each level in order. You can help your young reader improve and become more confident by encouraging his or her own interests and abilities. From books your child reads with you to the first books he or she reads alone, there are I Can Read Books for every stage of reading:

SHARED READING
Basic language, word repetition, and whimsical illustrations, ideal for sharing with your emergent reader

BEGINNING READING
Short sentences, familiar words, and simple concepts for children eager to read on their own

READING WITH HELP
Engaging stories, longer sentences, and language play for developing readers

READING ALONE
Complex plots, challenging vocabulary, and high-interest topics for the independent reader

ADVANCED READING
Short paragraphs, chapters, and exciting themes for the perfect bridge to chapter books

I Can Read Books have introduced children to the joy of reading since 1957. Featuring award-winning authors and illustrators and a fabulous cast of beloved characters, I Can Read Books set the standard for beginning readers.

A lifetime of discovery begins with the magical words **"I Can Read!"**

Visit www.icanread.com for information
on enriching your child's reading experience.

Superman: Pranking News
Copyright © 2016 DC Comics.
SUPERMAN and all related characters and elements are trademarks of and © DC Comics.
(s16)

HARP35008
Manufactured in U.S.A. No part of this book may be used or reproduced in any manner whatsoever without written permission except in the case of brief quotations embodied in critical articles and reviews. For information address HarperCollins Children's Books, a division of HarperCollins Publishers, 195 Broadway, New York, NY 10007.
www.harpercollinschildrens.com

Library of Congress Control Number: 2015950815
ISBN 978-0-06-236085-4

Book design by Victor Joseph Ochoa

16 17 18 19 20   LSCC   10 9 8 7 6 5 4 3 2
❖
First Edition

I Can Read!

SUPERMAN
PRANKING NEWS

by Donald Lemke

pictures by Patrick Spaziante

Superman created by Jerry Siegel and Joe Shuster
By special arrangement with the Jerry Siegel family.

HARPER

An Imprint of HarperCollinsPublishers

CLARK KENT

Clark Kent is a reporter at the *Daily Planet* newspaper. He is secretly Superman.

SUPERMAN

Superman, also known as the Man of Steel, has many amazing superpowers. Magic is one of his only weaknesses.

LOIS LANE

Lois Lane is a reporter at the *Daily Planet* newspaper. She works with Clark Kent.

THE *DAILY PLANET*

The *Daily Planet* is the largest newspaper in the city of Metropolis.

MR. MXYZPTLK

Mr. Mxyzptlk (pronounced Mix-yez-pittel-ik) is a magical man from the 5th Dimension. He loves to annoy Superman with his pranks.

Inside the Daily Planet Building,

Lois Lane typed a headline:

"Superman Saves the Day (Again)."

Fellow newspaper reporter

Clark Kent peered over her shoulder.

"Isn't that your fourth Superman

story this week?" he asked.

"Have any better ideas, Clark?"

Lois replied with a smirk.

Ka-boom!

A crack of thunder shook

the Daily Planet Building.

Lois and Clark ran to the window.

The sky above Metropolis blackened.

On the street stood a tiny man
wearing an orange suit and hat.
"Who's that?" Lois wondered aloud.
She turned toward Clark,
but he was nowhere to be found.

Out of sight, Clark quickly shed
his glasses, tie, and suit.
A red-and-blue uniform hid beneath.
Faster than lightning, he flew out
of the building as . . . Superman!

The Man of Steel had faced this

pest from the 5th Dimension before.

The pesky prankster loved to annoy

Superman with his magical powers.

The hero sighed. "Mr. Mxyzptlk."

"What are you doing here, Mxyzptlk?"

asked the Man of Steel.

"You've gotten a lot of attention

lately," Mxyzptlk explained.

"What better way to bother you

than stealing some of that thunder!"

Mxyzptlk lifted a bag toward the sky.

The clouds overhead swirled

into a giant tornado,

then funneled into the sack.

"This should make tomorrow's headlines," said Mr. Mxyzptlk. "Or at least the weather page!" The pesky pest tossed the sack toward the Daily Planet Building.

Fwoosh! Superman rocketed toward the bag at super-speed. He caught the sack in midair and wrapped it in his ultrastrong cape.

15

Ka-blam! The bag exploded
like a thousand thunderstorms.
The ground shook beneath
Superman's feet and the wind
swirled around his cape.

The wind whipped up an old
Daily Planet newspaper.

It floated into Mxyzptlk's hands.

The headline read:

"Superman, Person of the Year!"

"These stories are a bunch
of hot air!" shouted Mxyzptlk.
He twirled his hand at the
Daily Planet Building.
The building's rooftop globe
inflated like a hot-air balloon.
It floated into the sky,
lifting the building beneath it.
"Tee-hee!" Mxyzptlk laughed.

"Now that's what I call

a *sky*scraper!" said Mxyzptlk as

the building reached the clouds.

Superman soared into the sky.

The hero grabbed the building

and pulled with his super-strength.

Superman couldn't hold on for long.

He was unable to fight

Mr. Mxyzptlk's magical powers.

The Man of Steel thought fast.

He released the building and

flew toward the balloon.

"Time to bring this pest

down to Earth," thought Superman.

The super hero took a deep breath.

Fwoosh! He released a blast

of freeze breath at the globe.

The hot air inside the

globe quickly cooled.

It deflated like a leaky basketball.

The building slowly dropped back

to the ground with a *thud*!

Then Superman molded the building's
cracked steel and bricks
back together with his heat vision.
A crowd cheered for the super hero.

"News flash," said Mxyzptlk.

"I won't stop until everyone

knows my name!"

Only one thing could send the imp

back to the 5th Dimension.

Superman had to trick Mxyzptlk

into saying his name backward.

The super hero zoomed

into the Daily Planet Building.

Superman returned moments later.

He fought off Mxyzptlk's pranks

throughout the night.

At sunrise, a truck arrived with

the day's *Daily Planet* newspapers.

Superman quickly grabbed a copy.

"Look!" he told Mr. Mxyzptlk,

handing the pest a paper.

"You made the front page!"

"Really?" Mxyzptlk squealed.

Mxyzptlk grinned at his picture.

Then he spotted the headline:

"Mr. Kltpzyxm Gets Tricked!"

The pest looked puzzled.

"Who's Mr. Kltpzyxm?" he began, before realizing what he had said. Superman smiled as Mxyzptlk disappeared to the 5th Dimension. Metropolis was quiet once again.

Inside the Daily Planet Building,

Lois struggled for her next headline.

"Got any more brilliant

story ideas, Clark?" she asked.

"Sometimes, Lois," Clark told her,

"no news is good news."

Dear Parent:
Your child's love of reading starts here!

Every child learns to read in a different way and at his or her own speed. Some go back and forth between reading levels and read favorite books again and again. Others read through each level in order. You can help your young reader improve and become more confident by encouraging his or her own interests and abilities. From books your child reads with you to the first books he or she reads alone, there are I Can Read Books for every stage of reading:

SHARED READING
Basic language, word repetition, and whimsical illustrations, ideal for sharing with your emergent reader

BEGINNING READING
Short sentences, familiar words, and simple concepts for children eager to read on their own

READING WITH HELP
Engaging stories, longer sentences, and language play for developing readers

READING ALONE
Complex plots, challenging vocabulary, and high-interest topics for the independent reader

ADVANCED READING
Short paragraphs, chapters, and exciting themes for the perfect bridge to chapter books

I Can Read Books have introduced children to the joy of reading since 1957. Featuring award-winning authors and illustrators and a fabulous cast of beloved characters, I Can Read Books set the standard for beginning readers.

A lifetime of discovery begins with the magical words "I Can Read!"

Visit www.icanread.com for information
on enriching your child's reading experience.

Justice League: Battle of the Power Ring
Copyright © 2016 DC Comics.
JUSTICE LEAGUE and all related characters and elements are trademarks of and © DC Comics.
(s16)

HARP34441
Manufactured in the U.S.A.

Library of Congress catalog card number: 2015943578
ISBN 978-0-06-234494-6

Book design by Victor Joseph Ochoa

16 17 18 19 20   LSCC   10 9 8 7 6 5 4 3   ❖   First Edition

JUSTICE LEAGUE

BATTLE OF THE POWER RING

by Donald Lemke
pictures by Patrick Spaziante

HARPER
An Imprint of HarperCollinsPublishers

I Can Read!

READING 2 WITH HELP

GREEN LANTERN

Test pilot Hal Jordan is Green Lantern of Space Sector 2814. With his power ring, Green Lantern can create anything imaginable and guards Earth against the forces of evil.

SUPERMAN

Superman, also known as the Man of Steel, has many amazing superpowers. To hide his super hero identity, he works as reporter Clark Kent at the *Daily Planet* newspaper.

BATMAN

Orphaned as a child, young Bruce Wayne trained his body and mind to become Batman, the Dark Knight. He fights crime with high-tech gadgets and weapons.

THE FLASH

The Flash is also known as the Fastest Man Alive. With incredible speed, the lightning-quick super hero wastes no time taking down the world's worst villains.

DARKSEID

Darkseid is the ruler of the alien planet Apokolips and one of the most powerful beings in the universe.

DESAAD

Desaad is the chief scientist on Apokolips. He is also a loyal servant of Darkseid, ready to perform his master's evil deeds.

On Apokolips, the planet's ruler, Darkseid, sat atop his throne. His servant, Desaad, approached. "After years, I've finally done it, Lord Darkseid," said Desaad.

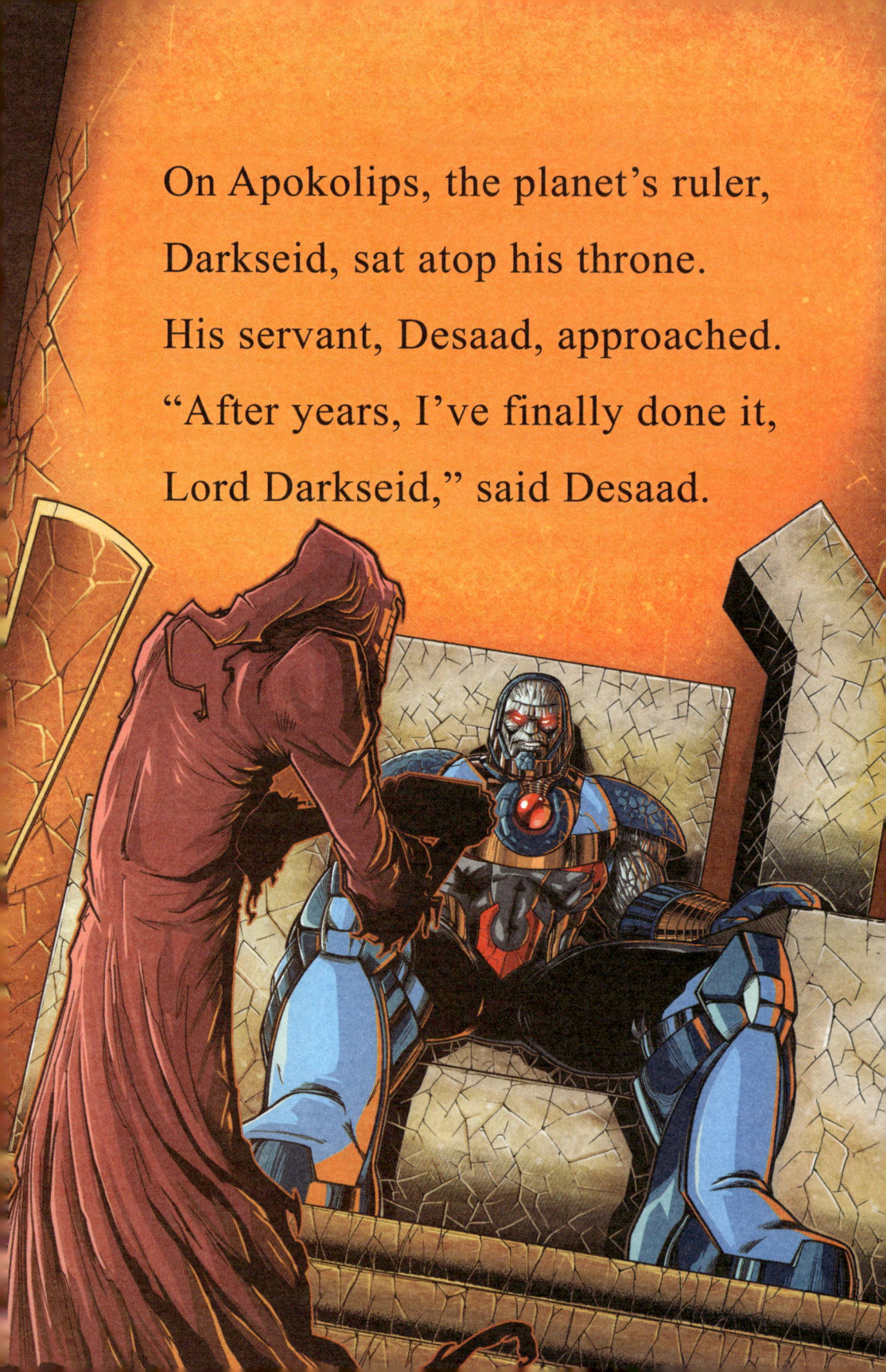

The servant held up a Mother Box.
A series of lights glowed on
the computer's small keypad.
"Behold, your newest weapon . . .
control of the Green Lanterns!"

"This device sends a signal to the planet Oa," Desaad said. "It then connects to the Galactic Guardians' computer, and I can control every power ring."

"Correction," growled Darkseid,
as he snatched the Mother Box
from his servant.

"*I* will control them."

Darkseid typed in a number: 2814.

On Earth, Hal Jordan sat inside
a fighter jet at Ferris Aircraft.
He reached for the jet's controls,
but his right hand wouldn't move.
His Green Lantern power ring glowed.
It suddenly had a mind of its own!

"Ready for takeoff, Jordan?" radioed the Ferris control tower. But before he could respond, the out-of-control ring pulled him from the cockpit and into the sky.

Miles away, reporter Clark Kent sat
inside the Daily Planet Building,
awaiting his next big scoop.
Suddenly his boss shouted,
"Coast City is under attack . . .
by Green Lantern!"

Out of sight, Clark shed his suit, revealing his Superman uniform. *ZOOM!* In a red-and-blue blur, the hero soared up, up, and away!

As Superman neared Coast City,
he saw Green Lantern high in the sky,
blasting the streets with his ring.
People fled in all directions.

14

"Hal!" shouted the Man of Steel.

"Hey, Superman," said Green Lantern.

"My ring is out of control!"

Suddenly the ring fired at Superman!

With his mighty fist, the super hero

shattered the green beam.

Just then, The Flash and Batman
arrived on the streets below.
"We thought you could use a hand,"
said the Fastest Man Alive.
"Another?" joked Hal. "I already
have one more than I can handle!"
An oversized cannon grew from
Green Lantern's out-of-control ring.
BOOM! It shot green cannonballs
at the Justice League members.

The Flash easily zigzagged
through the hail of cannonballs.
Batman fired his grapnel gun
at a nearby building,
zipping away from the explosions.

"Impressive," said a voice above.

The Justice League looked up.

"Darkseid," said Superman,

recognizing his worst enemy.

The villain floated above the city,

followed closely by Desaad.

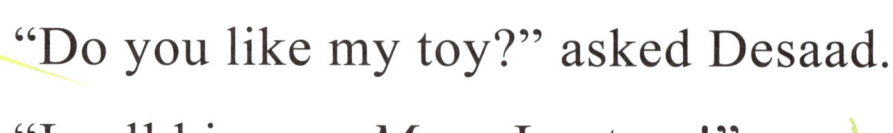

"Do you like my toy?" asked Desaad.

"I call him my *Mean* Lantern!"

"That has a nice ring to it,"
The Flash joked.

"I assure you," replied Darkseid,

"that ring is anything but nice."

Instantly the power ring formed
three heat-seeking missiles.
The super heroes fled as the bombs
exploded into nearby buildings.

"Look at them run!" Desaad laughed.
"They won't stand a chance against
our Green Lantern army."

"Correction," said Darkseid,
holding the Mother Box.

"*My* army."

Nearby, Green Lantern struggled with his out-of-control power ring. The ring struck him, over and over, with a giant green boxing glove. "Don't fight, mortal," Darkseid told him. "I'm your master now."

23

"You may control my ring," said Hal,
but you'll never control my will!"
Green Lantern removed his ring,
dropping the weapon at his feet.
Without its wearer, the power ring
quickly shut down.

"Fool!" cried Darkseid.

"You are nothing without that ring."

"Correction," said The Flash,

"He's a member of the Justice League."

The Flash darted at Darkseid,
landing fifty punches in a blink.
"No!" cried the evil ruler,
as the Mother Box fell from his hand.

"I don't have a ring," said Batman, "but these bracelets should fit." The Dark Knight held up a pair of shiny metal Bat-Cuffs. "Thanks, Batman," Hal said, "but green is more his color."

Green Lantern picked up
the Mother Box and typed in
a familiar number: 0000.
A Boom Tube to the planet Oa
opened behind the villains.

The Man of Steel flew at Darkseid.

WHAM! With a mighty punch,

he sent the villain into the tube,

and Desaad followed closely behind.

Green Lantern placed his
power ring back on his right hand.
The ring glowed under his control,
but Green Lantern didn't smile.
"What's wrong?" asked The Flash.

"My ring may be fixed," said Hal,

"but my reputation is ruined."

He pointed at frightened onlookers

and the smoldering city around them.

"Have no fear, Hal," Superman said. "Everyone will get the real scoop soon enough."

The Man of Steel zoomed away, heading back to the *Daily Planet*.

Dear Parent:
Your child's love of reading starts here!

Every child learns to read in a different way and at his or her own speed. Some go back and forth between reading levels and read favorite books again and again. Others read through each level in order. You can help your young reader improve and become more confident by encouraging his or her own interests and abilities. From books your child reads with you to the first books he or she reads alone, there are I Can Read Books for every stage of reading:

SHARED READING
Basic language, word repetition, and whimsical illustrations, ideal for sharing with your emergent reader

BEGINNING READING
Short sentences, familiar words, and simple concepts for children eager to read on their own

READING WITH HELP
Engaging stories, longer sentences, and language play for developing readers

READING ALONE
Complex plots, challenging vocabulary, and high-interest topics for the independent reader

ADVANCED READING
Short paragraphs, chapters, and exciting themes for the perfect bridge to chapter books

I Can Read Books have introduced children to the joy of reading since 1957. Featuring award-winning authors and illustrators and a fabulous cast of beloved characters, I Can Read Books set the standard for beginning readers.

A lifetime of discovery begins with the magical words **"I Can Read!"**

Visit www.icanread.com for information
on enriching your child's reading experience.

Batman: The Joker's Ice Scream
Copyright © 2015 DC Comics.
BATMAN and all related characters and elements are trademarks of and © DC Comics.
(s15)

HARP33533

Library of Congress catalog card number: 2014958856
ISBN 978-0-06-234492-2

Book design by Victor Joseph Ochoa

16 17 18 19 20   LSCC   10 9 8 7 6   ❖   First Edition

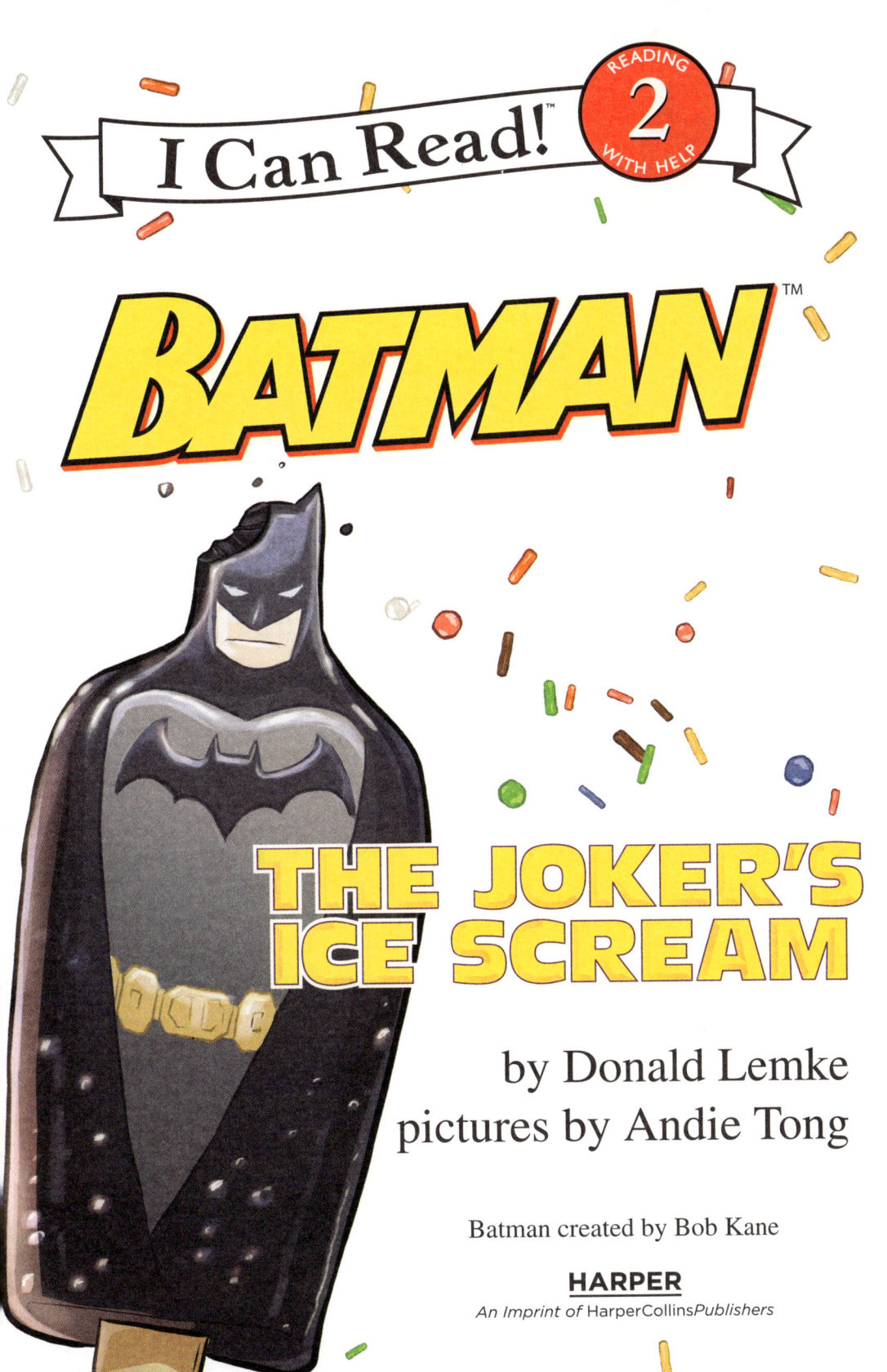

I Can Read!

READING WITH HELP 2

BATMAN™

THE JOKER'S ICE SCREAM

by Donald Lemke
pictures by Andie Tong

Batman created by Bob Kane

HARPER
An Imprint of HarperCollinsPublishers

BATMAN

Batman is an expert martial artist, crime fighter, and inventor. He is also known as the Dark Knight.

COMMISSIONER JAMES GORDON

James Gordon is the Gotham City Police Commissioner. He works with Batman to stop crime in the city.

BATGIRL

Barbara Gordon fights alongside Batman, using high-tech gadgets and martial arts skills. Her father, James Gordon, does not know her secret identity as Batgirl.

BATMOBILE

The Batmobile is Batman's high-tech vehicle. It is protected by armor and filled with dozens of weapons and gadgets.

THE JOKER

The Joker is Batman's enemy and one of the most dangerous villains in Gotham City. His nickname is the Clown Prince of Crime.

HARLEY QUINN

Former doctor Harleen Frances Quinzel is the Joker's girlfriend and partner in crime.

In the Gotham City Police station,
Commissioner James Gordon
wiped sweat from his forehead.
"Why's it so hot in here?" he asked.
"The air conditioner is broken
again, sir," answered an officer.

Gordon opened a nearby window.
The chimes of an ice cream truck
played on the street below.
"Time to cool off," he said
with a smile.

The green-and-purple truck
stopped in front of the station.
Painted on the side were two
big, bold words: ICE SCREAM!

A pale woman in a white hat greeted

the officers at the truck's window.

"What'll it be, boys?" she asked.

"I'll try a double scoop of

Vanilla Mean!" replied one officer.

"Kooky Dough for me!" said another.

The woman quickly served up

the ice cream with a straight face.

"Hey," said an officer,

"your sign says 'service with a smile.'"

He took a lick of his cone.

The woman removed her white hat.

"And you'll get what you paid for!" shouted Harley Quinn.
Suddenly the officer's mouth stretched into a wide, wicked grin.

Soon every officer was smiling
and laughing uncontrollably.
"Look, Mr. J!" said Harley.
"You finally gave the police
something to smile about!"

"*I* tell the jokes," yelled the Joker

from the driver's seat.

"Now let's roll.

By the end of today,

every cop in this city

will be eating out of our hands."

Batman arrived in downtown
Gotham City.
He stepped out of the Batmobile.
Empty ice cream cups
littered the sidewalk.

The Dark Knight kneeled next to
a half-eaten ice cream cone.
He removed a glass tube from
his Utility Belt and filled it
with some of the melted treat.
"Time to get the real scoop," he said.

Batman placed the tube

into a high-tech device

in the Batmobile.

The computer quickly identified

the formula: Joker Venom!

The poison left people with
a frozen smile and a craving
for more ice cream.

"If the Joker isn't stopped,"
said Batman, "the whole police force
will eat themselves silly!"

A few streets away,

the evil duo served up

their sweet treats.

Then Harley Quinn spotted the

Batmobile speeding toward them.

"It's Batman!" she cried.

The Joker pressed a large red button on the vehicle's dashboard.
In an instant, the ice cream truck changed into the Jokermobile.

The Joker led the Dark Knight on a
high-speed chase out of the city.
"He's gaining on us!" yelled Harley,
looking back at the Batmobile.
"I'll take care of him,"
said the Joker, "lickety-split!"

The villain pressed another button,
and the truck's rear doors opened.
Cherries, chocolate syrup, and bananas
spilled onto the road.

The Batmobile skidded in the
slippery sweets but stayed close.
"Time for seconds, Mr. J!"
Harley told her partner in crime.
"How about a little Rocky Road?"
the Joker said.
The villain steered the Jokermobile
onto a bumpy gravel road.
Soon the Batmobile was lost
in their dusty trail.

Suddenly a headlight appeared.

Batgirl blocked the road

on her Batcycle.

The hero flung a Batarang

at her enemies.

Boom! The Batarang exploded
in front of the Jokermobile.
"Look out, Mr. J!" cried Harley.
The truck crashed into the
explosion's cone-shaped crater.

Batman soon arrived at the scene.
"Thanks for helping me out
of a sticky situation," he said.
The heroes watched the villains
exit the Jokermobile.

Harley and the Joker were covered
from head to toe in ice cream!
"Looks like I'll be helping you
with another!" Batgirl laughed.

The heroes helped the evil duo
out of the pit.

"The joke's on you," said the Joker.

"The police still have a
case of brain freeze!"

Batgirl turned to the Dark Knight.

"He's right," she said.

"How will we get

the antidote to the police?"

"On a hot day like this," he said,

"it's always best to keep cool."

The Batmobile returned
to Gotham City,
towing the Jokermobile behind.
A hungry crowd
quickly surrounded them.

Harley and the Joker

served up their latest flavor.

It included a special ingredient:

the Joker Venom antidote!

Soon everyone was back to normal.

Batgirl zoomed off while Batman
spoke to the commissioner.
"Question," Gordon said.
"What do you call this flavor?"
"Batswirl," Batman said.
"A Dynamic Duo!"

Dear Parent:
Your child's love of reading starts here!

Every child learns to read in a different way and at his or her own speed. Some go back and forth between reading levels and read favorite books again and again. Others read through each level in order. You can help your young reader improve and become more confident by encouraging his or her own interests and abilities. From books your child reads with you to the first books he or she reads alone, there are I Can Read Books for every stage of reading:

SHARED READING
Basic language, word repetition, and whimsical illustrations, ideal for sharing with your emergent reader

BEGINNING READING
Short sentences, familiar words, and simple concepts for children eager to read on their own

READING WITH HELP
Engaging stories, longer sentences, and language play for developing readers

READING ALONE
Complex plots, challenging vocabulary, and high-interest topics for the independent reader

ADVANCED READING
Short paragraphs, chapters, and exciting themes for the perfect bridge to chapter books

I Can Read Books have introduced children to the joy of reading since 1957. Featuring award-winning authors and illustrators and a fabulous cast of beloved characters, I Can Read Books set the standard for beginning readers.

A lifetime of discovery begins with the magical words **"I Can Read!"**

Visit www.icanread.com for information
on enriching your child's reading experience.

Superman: A Giant Attack
Copyright © 2015 DC Comics.
SUPERMAN and all related characters and elements are trademarks of and © DC Comics.
(s15)

HARP33135
Manufactured in the U.S.A. No part of this book may be used or reproduced in any manner whatsoever without written permission except in the case of brief quotations embodied in critical articles and reviews. For information address HarperCollins Children's Books, a division of HarperCollins Publishers, 195 Broadway, New York, NY 10007.
www.harpercollinschildrens.com

Library of Congress catalog card number: 2014947578
ISBN 978-0-06-234488-5

Book design by Victor Joseph Ochoa

16 17 18 19 20   LSCC   10 9 8 7 6 5 4   ❖   First Edition

by Donald Lemke

pictures by Lee Ferguson

Superman created by Jerry Siegel and Joe Shuster
By special arrangement with the Jerry Siegel family.

HARPER
An Imprint of HarperCollinsPublishers

SUPERMAN

Superman, also known as the Man of Steel, has many amazing powers. He was born on the planet Krypton.

RED KRYPTONITE

A form of Kryptonite that has unexpected and temporary effects on Kryptonians.

S.T.A.R. LABS

S.T.A.R. Labs is a research facility located in Metropolis. Scientists at the laboratory invent high-tech weapons and gadgets.

LEX LUTHOR

Lex Luthor is a wealthy Metropolis businessman. He is Superman's enemy.

ZOD AND FAORA

Zod and Faora are criminals from Superman's home planet. They were sent to the Phantom Zone before Krypton was destroyed.

PHANTOM ZONE

The Phantom Zone is a prison dimension for criminals from Krypton. Prisoners travel to and from this prison through a Phantom Zone Projector.

DING! A golden elevator opened
on the top floor of LexCorp Tower.
Lex Luthor stepped out, and
a nervous scientist greeted him.
"Is everything ready?" Lex asked
the former S.T.A.R. Labs employee.

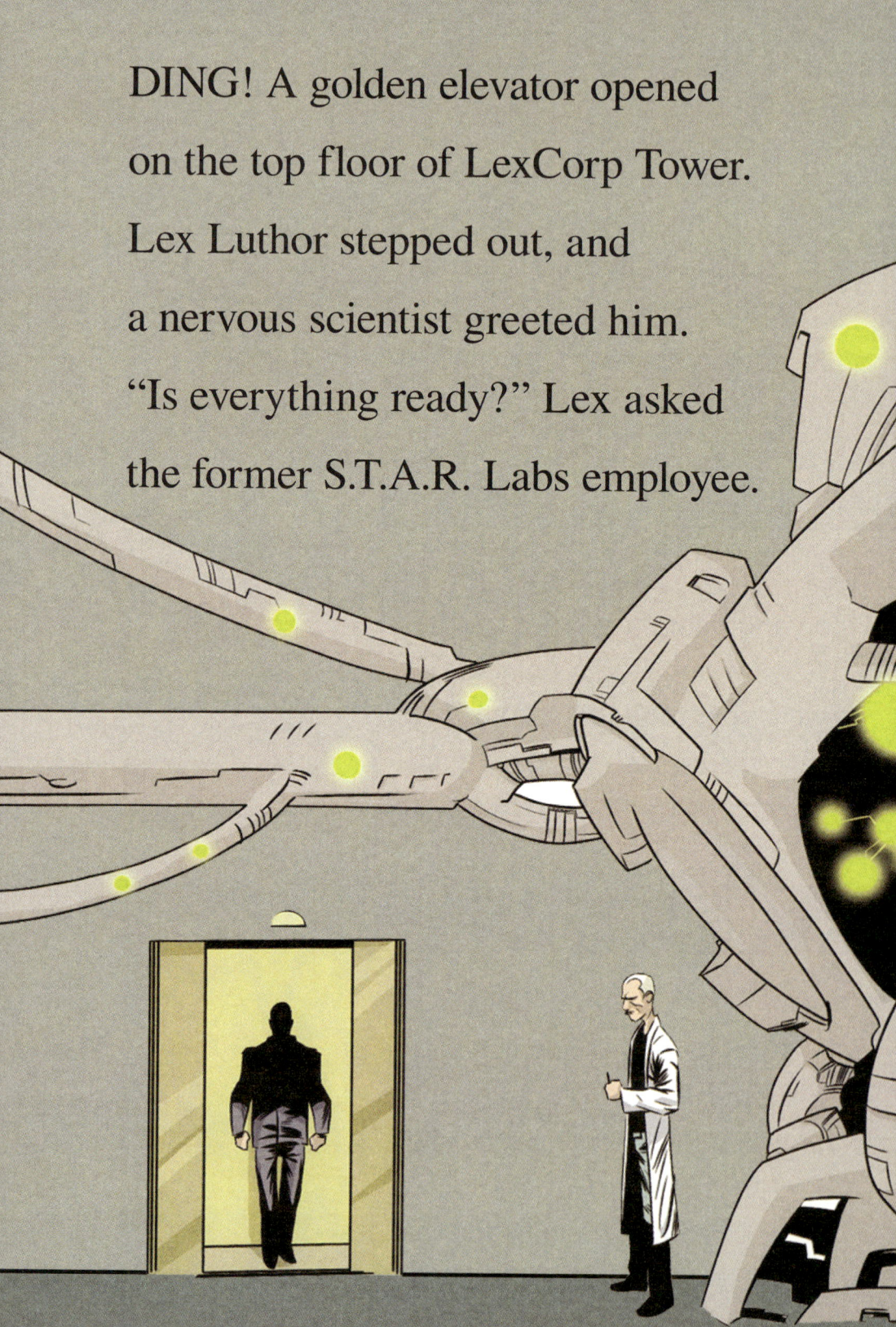

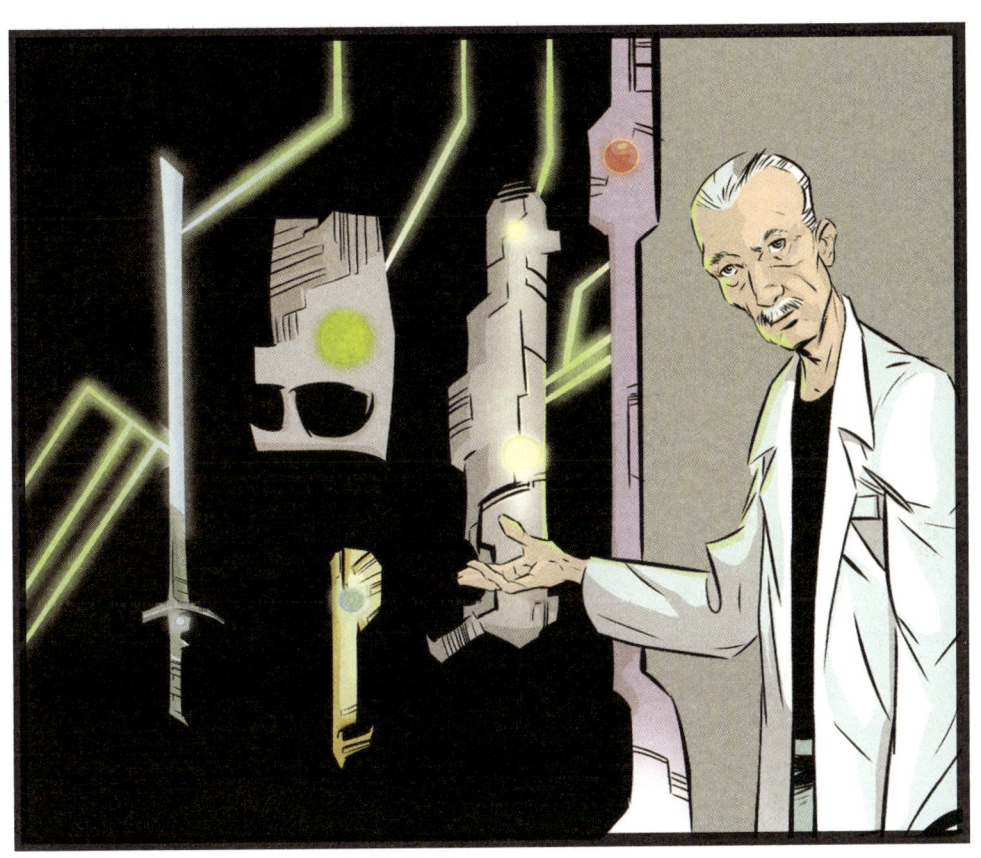

The scientist nodded and pointed
toward a large glass display case.
High-tech gadgets glowed inside.
Each device had one purpose:
to destroy Superman.

Lex removed a device from the case.

"A Phantom Zone Projector, sir,"

said the scientist.

"We built one at S.T.A.R. Labs.

Yours is better.

And more expensive."

Lex grabbed the scientist.

"I'd better get what I paid for,"

said the businessman.

Then he turned on the device.

BAM! Suddenly, two Phantom Zone

criminals appeared in front of them.

"Finally we're free!" said Zod.

"I wouldn't say 'free,'"
Lex told the criminals.

"What do you want?" asked Faora.

"Superman," he growled.

"Gladly," replied the evil duo.

"Excellent," said Lex,
grabbing a rocket launcher
from the case.

"Then meet me on the roof."

"Now what?" asked Faora.

Lex pointed the rocket launcher
toward the clear blue sky above.
"We start with a bang!" he said,
pulling the trigger.

KA-BOOM! A silver missile
streaked toward a nearby building.
Without delay, a blue-and-red figure
appeared beside it . . . Superman!

13

With super-speed, the Man of Steel
soared behind the missile
and grabbed the tail.
"Time to put the brakes on this
situation," the super hero said.

BLAM! The missile suddenly exploded in a blast of red light. The super hero fell from the sky, crashing through the thick concrete sidewalk below.

"What on earth is that weapon?"

Faora asked Lex.

"You won't find this weapon

on Earth," he replied.

"I've made the newest form

of Red Kryptonite."

On the ground below,

Superman grew . . . and grew!

"You fool!" shouted Zod.

"Do you know what kind of mess you've made?"

"A *giant* mess!" Faora answered.

The Man of Steel stood

taller than the LexCorp building.

The hero stared at the tiny

villains with his giant red eyes.

"You're all in big trouble,"

joked Superman.

Zod and Faora circled Superman's head
like two pesky bees.

"The bigger they are," Zod began.

"The harder they fall," added Faora.

The hero raised his huge palm.

"Bug off!" Superman shouted.

THWAP! He swatted
the villains in midair,
sending them crashing
into nearby buildings.

The evil duo flew

at Superman again.

They punched him over and over

with their teeny, pin-size fists.

"I'm growing tired of you two,"

Superman said, letting out a yawn.

A gust of super-breath

escaped his mouth.

The villains fell to the ground,

covered in a layer of ice.

Zod and Faora quickly flew back

to the LexCorp building.

"Get back out here!" cried Lex.

"You still owe me for your freedom!"

"Until that Red K wears off," said Faora,

"we'd be crazy to stay and fight him."

"Then our deal is dead," said Lex,
starting the Phantom Zone Projector.
With the push of a button, he sent
the evil duo back to their prison.

Superman's giant finger suddenly
smashed through a nearby window.
Lex hid behind the display case.
The super hero searched the room
with his X-ray vision.
He quickly spotted his enemy.

The Man of Steel blasted the case
with his heat vision. FWOOSH!
In an instant,
Lex's gadgets melted
into a red-hot puddle
on the floor.

"What have you done?" Lex asked
the scientist standing nearby.
"What you wanted, sir," he replied.
"How long will this last?" said Lex.
"If my Red K formula was correct,"
answered the scientist, "two days."

The giant Superman grabbed

Lex and the scientist.

"If we last that long," Lex added.

Superman pulled the men

into the air.

"S.T.A.R. Labs' secrets

are safe again," he said, smiling.

Suddenly the hero began shrinking.

Lex and the scientist dropped

to the rooftop.

Superman returned to normal size.

"This giant mess is all your fault!"
Lex shouted at the scientist
as a policeman led them away.
"Don't worry," said the super hero.
"You'll both pay for this mistake."

Dear Parent:
Your child's love of reading starts here!

Every child learns to read in a different way and at his or her own speed. Some go back and forth between reading levels and read favorite books again and again. Others read through each level in order. You can help your young reader improve and become more confident by encouraging his or her own interests and abilities. From books your child reads with you to the first books he or she reads alone, there are I Can Read Books for every stage of reading:

SHARED READING
Basic language, word repetition, and whimsical illustrations, ideal for sharing with your emergent reader

BEGINNING READING
Short sentences, familiar words, and simple concepts for children eager to read on their own

READING WITH HELP
Engaging stories, longer sentences, and language play for developing readers

READING ALONE
Complex plots, challenging vocabulary, and high-interest topics for the independent reader

ADVANCED READING
Short paragraphs, chapters, and exciting themes for the perfect bridge to chapter books

I Can Read Books have introduced children to the joy of reading since 1957. Featuring award-winning authors and illustrators and a fabulous cast of beloved characters, I Can Read Books set the standard for beginning readers.

A lifetime of discovery begins with the magical words **"I Can Read!"**

Visit www.icanread.com for information on enriching your child's reading experience.

Superman: Superman Versus Bizarro
SUPERMAN and all related characters and elements are trademarks of DC Comics © 2010. All rights reserved.
Manufactured in U.S.A. No part of this book may be used or reproduced in any manner whatsoever without written permission except in the case of brief quotations embodied in critical articles and reviews. For information address HarperCollins Children's Books, a division of HarperCollins Publishers, 195 Broadway, New York, NY 10007.
www.icanread.com

Library of Congress catalog card number: 2009930271
ISBN 978-0-06-188516-7
Book design by John Sazaklis

16 17 18 19 20   LSCC   10   ❖   First Edition

I Can Read!

READING
2
WITH HELP

SUPERMAN

Superman
Versus Bizarro

by Chris Strathearn
pictures by MADA Design, Inc.

SUPERMAN created by Jerry Siegel and Joe Shuster

HARPER
An Imprint of HarperCollinsPublishers

CLARK KENT

Clark Kent
lives in Metropolis.
He is secretly Superman.

LOIS LANE

Lois Lane is a
newspaper reporter.
She writes a lot
about Superman.

BIZARRO

Bizarro looks
a lot like Superman,
but he has opposite powers.

SUPERMAN

Superman has many amazing powers. He was born on the planet Krypton.

BIZARRO WORLD

Bizarro comes from a planet called Bizarro World. It is a lot like Earth, except that everything is backward.

One morning in Metropolis,

Clark Kent was walking to work.

The streets were crowded and noisy

with the sounds of cars and people.

Clark heard something else.

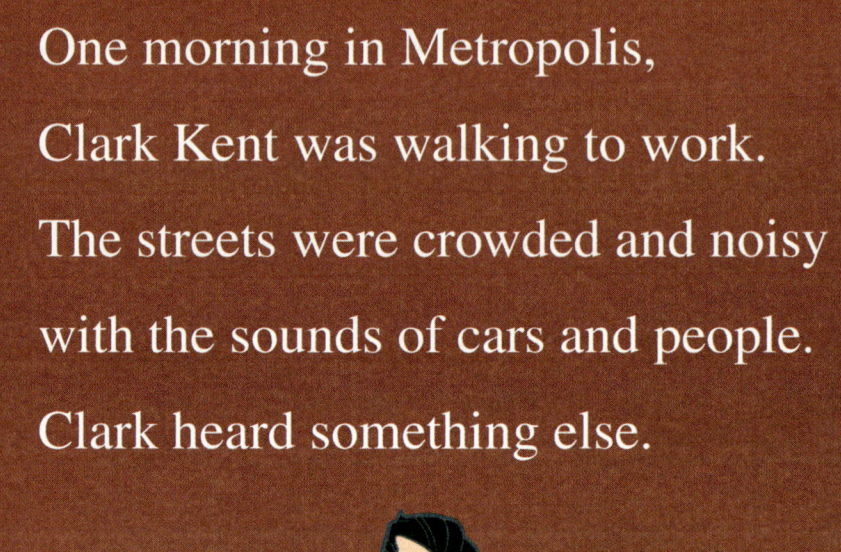

Clark could hear a scared cat

cry from far away.

Clark stepped into an alley

and changed into his costume.

"This is a job for Superman!"

The cat was stuck high in a tree.

Superman swooped down to help,

but someone was already there!

Under the tree was a strange man.

It was Superman's backward clone!

His name was Bizarro.

"The kitty is scaring the tree!"

shouted Bizarro.

"Bizarro must save the tree!"

Bizarro grabbed the tree trunk

and pulled it from the ground.

CRASH!

Bizarro was powerful but clumsy.

"Bizarro is the best hero!"

said Bizarro as he flew off.

"I should follow him to make sure

he won't save anything else!"

said Superman.

Superman followed Bizarro
all the way to a burning warehouse.
"Bizarro will help the firemen!"
said Bizarro.

Bizarro lifted a fire truck over his head.

"Fire trucks put out fires!" he said.

"Wait!" said Superman.

Bizarro didn't wait.

He tossed the truck at the fire.

It crashed and exploded!

"Done!" said Bizarro.

14

Once again, Bizarro flew away,
but the fire was still burning!
Superman quickly blew out the flames
with jets of icy air.

"Does Bizarro think he's a hero?"

Lois Lane asked Superman

after he put out the fire.

"Yes," said Superman,

"but his thinking is backward

because he is from Bizarro World.

Bizarro must return to his own planet."

"Please make him leave before

he destroys Metropolis!" Lois said.

Superman heard new cries for help.

A boat was sinking in the river.

There was no time to lose.

Superman had to get there before Bizarro!

Bizarro was already at the boat.

"No problem!" said Bizarro.

"The river is hurting the boat,

so Bizarro will stop the river!"

Bizarro knocked down a bridge.

CRASH! SPLASH! WHOOSH!

Pieces of rock and steel

piled up high in the river.

Superman picked up the boat
and flew it to safety.

Now the river was overflowing.
It was going to flood the city!

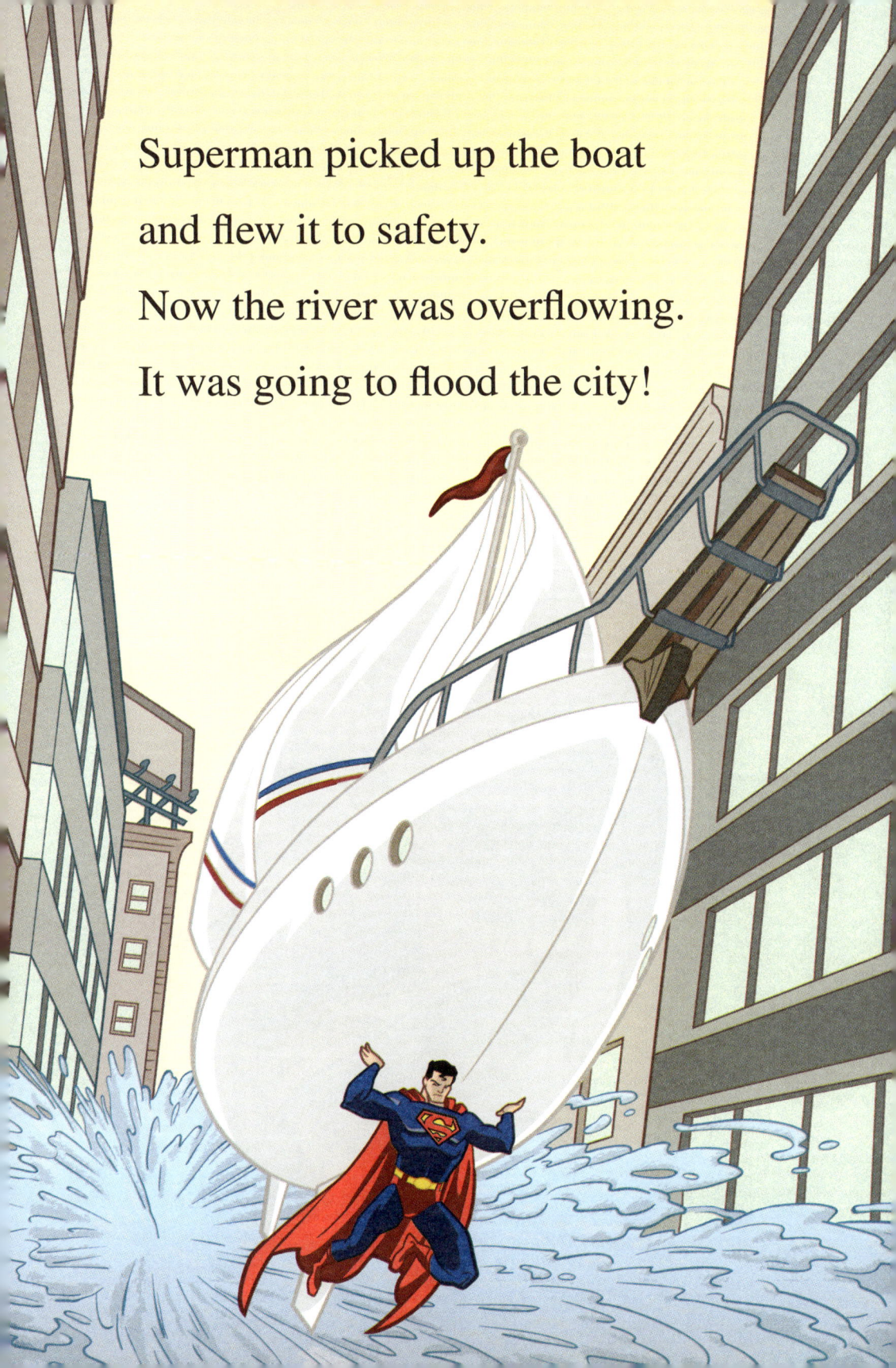

With super-speed and super-strength,
Superman moved the rocks and steel
that blocked the river.

Water began to flow once more.

"Now to rebuild the bridge!" he said.

Superman used his heat rays

to weld the bridge back together.

Bizarro was angry at Superman.

"What are you doing?" he yelled.

"Bizarro is the hero,

not Superman!" Bizarro yelled.

Superman faced Bizarro.

"Bizarro, you can't stay on Earth!

It's time for you to go home!"

Bizarro stomped his feet.

The ground trembled and shook.

"No!" he shouted.

"Superman should leave Metropolis!"

Bizarro threw a statue at Superman.

Superman dodged the statue,

but Bizarro attacked again.

He shot freeze rays from his eyes.

Superman was covered in ice.

"Ha!" laughed Bizarro.

"Superman is not so hot anymore!"

Superman easily broke free.

"Bizarro, look around you!"
Superman pointed at the mess.
"You can't fix anything on Earth.
Your backward thinking is good
only on Bizarro World!"

Bizarro suddenly grew quiet.

He knew Superman was right.

"Bizarro is tired of Earth, anyway.

It is too backward here," he said.

"If I'm needed here," said Superman,

"you must be needed on your world."

This cheered Bizarro up.

"Bizarro is a big hero over there!"

he said proudly.

Bizarro turned and flew away.

He left Earth for Bizarro World

and the Bizarro people who needed him.

Back on Bizarro World,

a woman cried out.

"Help! Kitty is hurting the tree!"

Bizarro knew just what to do.